It was supposed to be a relaxing vacation in the Caribbean, with a scoop of a story to boot, but it wasn't supposed to be dangerous…

Mark took a notebook out of his pocket. He wanted to make a few notes—and capture a few questions and ideas before they disappeared from his head. When the bartender looked his way, Mark signaled that he was ready for another cold beer.

He was still writing when the beer arrived, and, as he lifted the bottle, he saw that a piece of paper was stuck to the bottom. He thought it was just something left from the bar, but he noticed there was writing on it. He was curious, and then surprised, and then angry when he read the message. *This ain't any if your business. Don't try to make it any. For everyone's good, leave it alone—and leave the island—NOW*.

He looked around quickly to see if he could figure out who had written it. No one was looking his way. There wasn't a clue who sent it.

He took only a fast sip of the beer, put some money on the table, stood up, and left quickly. He had a bad feeling about this whole thing. It wasn't just about crazy water. There was much more going on. He didn't have a clue what it could be, but something was wrong.

Investigative reporter Mark Williams and his marine biologist wife Flo are trying to decide where to go on vacation when they get a frantic phone call from one of Flo's old professors who now lives in the Bahamas. He begs Flo and Mark to join him in Bimini, promising new scientific discoveries for Flo and a breaking-story scoop for Mark. Intrigued, the couple fly to meet Professor Delta in Bimini. But what they find when they get there is a lot more than they had bargained for—in fact, it could cost them their lives…

KUDOS for *Bermuda Sounds*

In *Bermuda Sounds* by J. Robert Parkinson, Mark and Flo Williams are trying to decide on where to go on vacation when Flo gets a frantic phone call from an old professor who is now in Bimini. Professor Delta believe he is on the verge of a breakthrough scientific discovery, but he wants Flo, who is also a scientist., to go over his data and check his fact to see if she reaches the same conclusion. Flo is hesitant, as this was supposed to be a vacation, so Delta sweetens the pot, promising that her reporter husband Mark will get an exclusive scoop on the discovery. So Mark and Flo head to Bimini. When they arrive, they discover the professor has stumbled onto something that some powerful people don't want exposed, and if they aren't careful, it could cost all of them their lives. The story is fast-paced and intense, the plot strong, and even the science is plausible. I thoroughly enjoyed it. ~ *Taylor Jones, The Review Team of Taylor Jones & Regan Murphy*

Bermuda Sounds by J. Robert Parkinson is the story of a scientist who discovers something he shouldn't. Professor Delta lives in Bimini, and he thinks he knows the secret to the Bermuda Triangle. He calls a former colleague, Flo Williams, and asks her to fly to Bimini to double check his data and make sure his conclusions are sound. When Flo hesitates, Delta promises her that her husband, who's an investigative report, will have the story of the century when the discovery is unveiled. When Mark and Flo arrive in Bimini, the science seems to check out. At least in the lab, but when the trio decide to test their theory on the open ocean, they run into far more than rough water. The secret of the Bermuda Triangle seems to be a secret that some powerful people don't want exposed, and they will do anything to stop it. I like the story, and the theories presented make a lot of sense. Parkinson combines, mystery, science, and suspense to create an intriguing, thought-provoking, and entertaining tale. Very well done.

~ *Regan Murphy, The Review Team of Taylor Jones & Regan Murphy*

ACKNOWLEDGMENTS

I am indebted to many people for this book.

First of all, to my SCUBA diving "buddies" for their instruction and support.

Then to a stranger who "planted" the seed for this story during an informal conversation during a dive trip in the Caribbean many years ago.

To Faith who edited the manuscript and turned it into a book.

To Jack for using his artistic skills to create the cover.

Thanks to all.

BERMUDA SOUNDS

J. Robert Parkinson, PhD

A Black Opal Books Publication

BERMUDA SOUNDS
Copyright © 2017 by J. Robert Parkinson, PhD
Cover Design by J. Robert Parkinson
All cover art copyright © 2017
All Rights Reserved
Print ISBN: 978-1-626947-89-4

First Publication: NOVEMBER 2017

Published by Black Opal Books **http://www.blackopalbooks.com**

DEDICATION

To my wife, Eileen
my first editor
and my greatest supporter

and

To my son, Robert, and to my daughter, Enid,
for their ongoing interest.

They make it all worthwhile.

CHAPTER 1

Mark and Flo Williams were figuring out where to go on vacation. They had been married for a little more than four years, and this was the first chance they had to get away.

When they had finished college, each followed a different career path, and both achieved a level of success, although neither was where he or she wanted to be yet.

They met after graduation, and it was a case of opposite attraction. He was a gregarious investigative reporter and moved slowly up the ranks of the news business, but she preferred "Alone Time" in a laboratory.

Now they just wanted to get away for a little while, and they were studying travel brochures.

Mark was a TV reporter working for a Washington, DC station as a street reporter. He didn't expect to become an anchorman for some time—if ever. He was good on the street, but didn't have the personality or the presence—or the drive—to make it to an anchor spot.

Flo, on the other hand, was driven. As a marine biologist, she worked in applied research at the National Aquarium in Baltimore. She joined the staff there after completing a successful research project at Woods Hole. With a PhD tucked under her belt, she taught in the Marine Biology Department at San Diego State. Her work there was what brought her to the attention of the people at Woods Hole and to Dr. Ron Delta, with whom she would work closely before moving to The National Aquarium.

The worst part of winter was finally over, and Mark and Flo both had time off coming. Washington could be a terrible place to live in winter because no one seemed to know how to drive—and wasn't inclined to learn. As soon as there was an inch of snow on the ground traffic stopped, and drivers seemed to become stupid.

Mark and Flo were ready for a break, but as was often the case, they couldn't come to an agreement about a location.

Flo held up a brochure. "Spelunking."

"No way. Let's get out of here and see some real snow. Not this dirty stuff. Skiing will be good for both of us, Flo."

"You just want to see all those little snow bunnies in their tight pants."

"Yeah, like the ones you wear."

"Thanks for that, but soft talk won't work."

Mark just shook his head. "You can't blame a guy for trying. But why would you want to crawl around in a cave on your hands and knees when you can look at the sun and the mountains?'

"I don't know. Maybe it's because my mother made me stay so clean when I was little. And in the lab, everything is clean. I'm ready for something dirty."

"I like the dirty part, but when I was a kid, I was filthy all the time. Now I prefer the clean air and the mountains."

"Well, I don't want to travel a thousand miles just to get cold and wet in the snow."

Mark gave a shrug. "Maybe someplace we can find a mountain with a cave," he murmured. "But look, we have three weeks' vacation coming with nothing to do, so let's find the right 'nothing' and get started."

"Maybe the Encyclopedia can help."

Mark picked up volume one and read "Afghanistan?"

"Too dangerous. Too hot."

"Alaska?"

"Too cold."

"Brazil?"

"Too many little string bikinis for you to handle."

Mark leered. "I'd like to try."

It was pretty clear this was going nowhere, and they were saved by a ringing telephone. Mark answered.

"Yes. Yes, she's here. Can I tell her who's calling? Okay. Just a minute." With a frown, he handed the phone to Flo. "It's for you. Professor something. Something about an airplane. He sounds excited—or high. I guess excited is better."

Flo put the receiver up to her ear. "Hello." A pause, then she exclaimed with excitement, "Professor Delta!" She shot an annoyed look at Mark for that childish remark about airplanes. "What a surprise! How are you?" She looked at Mark. "It's my oceanography professor from grad school," she said then turned back to the phone. "What are you doing? You sound as if something terrific just happened."

Flo heard Professor Delta take a deep breath then start talking so fast she had trouble following him.

"Flo, I think I've made a real discovery, but it's so simple on the surface, I need a tough mind and a pair of sharp eyes to check my findings. I need you. I need you to check my data. I want to be absolutely certain about these findings. Take no chances. No errors. No bad press."

CHAPTER 2

When he taught at the university level, Professor Delta always had others to check his work and to challenge his findings. An appropriate academic activity. Now after being on the faculty of MIT for two decades, he was working alone.

His discipline was physics, and he did extensive work in the field of audio transmission and sound wave research. He had become interested in the methods and effects of sound transmission in the ocean after reading how some whales were distracted and disoriented by sounds coming from submarines. Those audio distractions caused a great deal of conflict between the military and the ecologists. The later didn't want anyone or anything to interfere with "Mother Nature," but national security was the primary focus of the navy. While the ecologists wanted to have everything untouched, the military had to protect and defend national safety and interests.

Such differences were bound to clash, and conflicts were regular events. Protecting resources and using them were sometimes poles apart.

It was Delta's marine research that provided him the opportunity to meet Flo. At that time, she was still Flo Cooper. The relationship was always professional. When Flo was his young graduate assistant, he was already in his early sixties and a bit overweight for his five-foot-ten-inch stature.

On the university campus, he always had other professional colleagues to question, test, and reassure him about his work and his findings, but that was all gone now. He had left academia and was working on his own. While that freedom gave him the flexibility to select his own areas of research with no one interfering, he came to realize he needed the support and the questioning of colleagues, as well as the financial support that came easily through a university connection. Now, as a solo researcher, it was more difficult to attract funding. His track record was good, however, and he had been able to secure two multiple-year research contracts. At the moment, financial support wasn't a problem.

He was always capable, but, in some circumstances, he wasn't confident.

Even as his graduate student, Flo was able to probe, define, challenge, and then support his research. There was never any question that he was the primary intellect behind his work, but Flo was able to help him define it. She never attempted to claim unmerited status, and her career grew because of his reputation.

They began as teacher/student, became colleagues, and then friends.

From the tone of his voice, Flo could tell this was a call from a friend in need—from a fellow-scientist with something to share and to question.

He long ago gave up thinking about his academic "glory days," but he evidently continued to work for the sake of the work itself. The academic and the scientist continued looking for answers—and the questions kept coming.

As in his younger days, when he caught an idea, he held on for all it was worth. He sometimes knew things, but wasn't always sure of what he knew.

That was why the call to Flo.

CHAPTER 3

Mark was looking at the phone, getting impatient—and a bit annoyed—because of the avoidance behavior.

"Where are you? What have you done?" asked Flo.

Delta lowered his voice, like characters do in movies when they don't want unwelcome ears to hear them. "I can't talk about it on the phone."

Flo thought, but didn't say, *Then why did you call me?*

"You've got to get down here. I'm in Bimini—in the Bahamas."

Again she thought, *I know where it is.* Then she sighed. "I can't. Mark and I can't just jump down there. We've been making plans for a vacation trip to—someplace."

"Make this that 'someplace,'" Delta said quickly. "Come here to help. You won't regret it. It could be great for your career, and you can get a good suntan at the same time. And it won't cost you anything! Come on. It could also be good for Mark's career, too. He's still a reporter, isn't he?"

"He is, but what does that have to do with me looking at your data?"

"Flo, if what I think is true about what I've found out, there'll be plenty to report about. He could even get a…what do you call it?…a real poop. Scoop. Something like that."

"Scoop!" With hesitation and a bit of worry, Flo shot a quick glance at Mark. "I don't know, Professor. This is so unexpected. And we have so much on our plates already. Can we think about it for a little bit? Can I call you back?"

"Sure," Professor Delta answered with a sense of urgency, "but don't take too long. This is big, and I'm not even sure yet just how big. I think I've found the key to a long-time secret. I want to move fast before I miss this chance—and before anything else goes wrong. Take all the time you want—then call me back in an hour."

With that, Delta hung up. Flo stared at the phone for a moment. The man on the phone certainly sounded like Professor Delta. She was sure of that, but she had never heard him so excited—and, at the same time, so worried.

Whatever it was, she was sure it had to be important to make him act like this.

During the phone call, Mark had been looking at the travel section of the newspaper. The encyclopedia had more information about possible locations than they wanted or needed. He looked at Flo. "What was that all about?"

"He wants me—us—to fly to Bimini in the Caribbean, right away. He says he's discovered something really big. He wants me to check his data to be sure."

Mark put down the paper. "That's okay for you, but what do you mean he wants 'us'?"

"That's what he said. He said there could be a scoop for you—" With a grin she corrected herself. "—actually, he said there could be a poop for you, but he meant to say scoop. He's sure it could be good for your career as well as mine."

"Did he give you any indication what it was?" Mark asked, now with a bit on interest. "Anything at all to go on?"

She looked at the phone. "No, just that it was big." She paused. "But he was excited, and that's not like him at all. I've known him for a long time, and he has always been the detached scientist. No emotion. Only facts. This is very unlike him." Another pause, this time a long one, and Flo shrugged. "What do you think? Should we go? It could solve our problem about a vacation plan. We could get some of that 'fun in the sun' people talk about. Maybe even learn something at the same time. I could do some research, visit with my old mentor. And you could get a poop. I mean a story—a scoop. And the price is right. It'll be free, and we'll even make some money at the same time."

Mark stood up. "Why not? We couldn't figure this out on our own, and your professor handed us a solution. And a free vacation. What could be wrong with that? Call him back. Tell him we're on our way."

Flo was now starting to see the excitement in the opportunity. "Okay. Let's get out the bathing suits and start packing."

Taking a few steps toward Flo, Mark grinned. "Right. Get out that new little one you recently bought. Just in case the professor doesn't make his great discovery, we can do a little exploring on our own. I'll lead the safari. Do they have safaris in the Caribbean?"

Flo playfully pushed him away. "Don't get carried away. Call the airlines to see when we can get a flight. Then I'll call Professor Delta and tell him he can expect us. He's really something else, ya' know. I've been out of his classes for years, and he still makes me jump when he calls."

Mark already was dialing the phone, calling a travel agency. "Hello," he said when an agent answered. "I want to make reservations for two from Baltimore to Bimini." He paused to listen. "Tonight if that's possible."

Another pause. He looked at his watch. "That's great. We'll be there. Williams, Mr. and Mrs.—Mark and Florence. No we can't schedule a return yet. Thanks. Bye." He hung up the phone, turned to Flo. "Three hours and we'll be on our way. We should arrive at six a.m. tomorrow."

Flo picked up the phone. "I'll call Professor Delta, and let him know we'll be there in the morning."

Mark nodded. "I'll start getting our stuff ready."

CHAPTER 4

The sun was already up as the plane circled to set up the final approach to the runway on Bimini. Flo and Mark quickly finished a small cup of coffee, working hard to wake up.

Night flights allowed for sleeping, but it never seemed to be a restful sleep.

Passengers tended to wake up groggy, and a touch on the irritable side. Both Mark and Flo tried to put on a good face as they collected their belongings.

The plane landed smoothly and the pilot taxied to the small terminal building.

At the "Bing" of the seat belt bell, the head flight attendant held up a hand. "All rise" she said, just as a bail-iff in a courtroom did when the judge entered.

And everyone stood up—right on cue. Laughing at themselves for their silly behavior, they exited the plane and walked to the terminal building.

After collecting their luggage and going through Customs—fortunately with no delays because the agents looked like they, too, were sleepy at this hour—Mark and Flo walked outside, looking for a familiar face. They didn't see one.

Professor Delta wasn't there.

A "local" approached them. "Are you Ms. Flo Cooper?"

"Used to be. Now the name is Williams." She turned to Mark with a frown. "How about that? He calls to ask an important favor then he forgets my name!"

Mark took her arm. "Easy. You said he was excited about something. Maybe he just has a lot to think about and his internal clock went back to your classroom days. No big deal."

"We'll see." And Flo turned back to the stranger.

"I'm Alvin," the man said. "Professor Delta sent me to get you. To take you to his home. He is sorry he couldn't come for you himself, but he said you would understand." Puzzled, he looked at Flo. "Do you?"

"Oh yes. I understand," Flo replied with a big exhale. "Just like the old days." She turned to Mark. "He gets everybody else to do things—to jump through hoops like we did last night—but he doesn't."

Trying to get her to unwind, Mark smiled. "It's okay. Take it easy. He probably made another great discovery. More research for you—and a poop for me."

She laughed, and they all walked to Alvin's car. He put their bags into the trunk and fastened the lid closed with a frayed bungee cord. "All set. Let's go."

The dilapidated car looked as if it had been driven hard for a long time and maybe even shipped here to the island from the States years ago.

The beat-up road was a good match for the equally beat-up car, but once they were away from the airport the scenery took their attention. It was beautiful here! As they drove along the ocean road they saw exotic, colorful birds, a couple of dolphins playing in the bay, and big surf.

"Paradise," Flo said and squeezed Mark's hand. "I'm glad we did this."

Mark squeezed back. "Me too."

CHAPTER 5

Finally, Alvin pulled up to Professor Delta's house. Although only one story, it was much bigger than they expected. A fine house, but not ostentatious. Louvered shutters covered every window, keeping out the sun but allowing plenty of space for the breezes to get inside.

The overhanging eves provided plenty of shade, as well as atmosphere. The house wasn't air conditioned so shade and breeze were necessary for comfort. A large covered porch surrounded the entire house, and it was fitted with a varied collection of rocking chairs. Inviting! Behind the house was another building, smaller and equally well kept. Both Mark and Flo guessed it was the laboratory.

Just as they reached the top step on the porch, the big door flew open, and Professor Delta appeared. "Flo, Mark. Glad to see you." He hugged Flo and shook hands with Mark. "How are you? Did you have a good flight? Are you hungry? Thirsty?" He never gave them a chance to answer any of the questions. "Come in. I'm so glad you're here."

Both of them responded at the same time, attempting to answer all of the Prof's questions at once. "Okay. Us, too. Sure. Fine."

The professor stopped Alvin, touching his arm. "Will you please take their things to their room?" And then he turned back to Flo and Mark. "And the two of you, please come with me to the Lab. I have much to show you."

No time wasted here. Flo thought and looked quizzically at Mark.

"This must be important, Flo," Mark said.

"It is," was all that Delta said.

As they headed back out to the porch, Mark pushed one of the rockers and said to it, "I guess we'll have to wait to visit with you. Maybe later. With a big cool drink. Save us a place."

Walking fast, Professor Delta led them around to the rear of the house, toward the smaller building. "I can't tell you how glad I am to see you here."

"Mark and I are glad to be here, but what's the big find you want me to look at?"

"In a minute—In a minute. Mark are you ready for your big story?"

"Yeah," Mark replied, trying to slow the pace a bit. "But even if you don't have a big scoop for me, I'm looking forward to a great vacation. Your call came just in time. We were having a serious discussion and a problem deciding where to go and what to do." He smiled. "You know, you might have saved our marriage."

Absently, as if he wasn't really interested, Professor Delta nodded. "That's good. But now to work."

When they entered the lab, Flo and Mark were overwhelmed with the amount and the variety of equipment they saw. Their first reaction was that it was like looking at a classic horror movie with all the vials, generators, test tubes, microphones, monitors, speakers, tanks, and other scientific "stuff."

With soundproofing on the walls, the place looked a bit like a recording studio or a radio station. Either Professor Delta was going into the music business, or he was doing research on some kind of high-tech sound production.

Going into the music business seemed unlikely, so Flo and Mark looked at each other and shrugged their shoulders.

"What is all this?" Flo asked.

"In a minute. First, please sit down. There's plenty to eat and drink here. You must be hungry after your flight."

Professor Delta gestured toward the overflowing table. "Please, help yourself. What I have to tell you could take a few minutes, so get comfortable."

They were both hungry and thirsty because the airline provided nothing other than a seat and a little cup of coffee, and even that was sparse. They both filled plates with small sandwiches and fresh fruit and sat on high stools placed at the lab table.

"Okay, Professor," Flo said, breaking the silence. "Now, what is this 'big discovery' you wanted to tell us about? Your phone call was intriguing enough to get us here in a hurry, now tell us. It must be really big for you to be this enthusiastic."

"It is!" He sat down at the lab table across from them. With a low and soft voice, he looked at them and grinned. "I think I've discovered the secret of the Bermuda Triangle."

CHAPTER 6

Mark was lifting a sandwich to his mouth but stopped with his hand in mid-air. "The *what*?"

"The Bermuda Triangle. We're right in the middle of it—and I know what causes all those strange events. I can explain the 'Unexplainable!' At least, I think I can. That's why I wanted you here, Flo. The answer seems so simple that I need someone—you—to check all of my data. As a student and as an assistant you always questioned everything I said and did in the classroom. Now I need that same questioning in the real world. You used to annoy me sometimes in the past, but now I really need your challenging questions and your skepticism before I announce my findings."

Mark put down his plate of fruit. "If what you said is true, you really are on to something big!"

"No wonder you sounded excited," Flo added.

Mark stood up from the stool, looking around the lab. "What a story it'll make for me. Can I use your phone to call Washington? This is really big!"

"Not so fast, Mark. Like I said, I *think* I found the secret, but I need to have Flo check my findings—and my interpretations."

Flo nodded. "Of course I will. I'm floored that you called me for the job. It's great! It's an honor."

"Well, like I said, you always questioned me. Now I need that same kind of questioning before I publish my results. I don't want to risk looking like a fool if I'm wrong."

Mark was now pacing around the lab, unable to sit still. "Tell us, Professor, what did you find that opened this door and got you so excited?"

Flo was now also standing. "I had no idea you were doing research on the Bermuda Triangle. That's so far from your field."

"That's the most interesting part. I wasn't doing research on anything. It just happened! Suddenly the answer was right in front of me. Everything I had read about the Triangle suddenly made sense. There was no more mystery!"

Mark couldn't contain himself. "Okay, okay. Tell us!"

"Yes, tell us. What's the secret?"

Professor Delta looked at each of them then focused on Flo. "Sound."

"Huh? Sound?" both Mark and Flo repeated.

"What do you mean?" Flo asked.

"Yes. Sound. Plain old sound waves. The same things that allow you to hear me talking to you right now. Sound waves!"

CHAPTER 7

You're going to have to give us a little more than that, Professor. How can sound waves cause all of that crazy stuff in the Triangle?"

"I think we need more, too. Professor," Flo chimed in. "A lot more!"

"I know. I know. Let me explain. Give me a minute to show you." The professor placed a disc in a video player and turned on the TV set. "Remember these events?" he asked as he turned on the player.

The video displayed footage of airplanes that had disappeared, boats that had sunk, compass readings going wild, etc. These were all classic examples of phenomena that defined the strange events of the Bermuda Triangle over many years.

"I remember most of that, but what about your

idea?" Mark said, still watching the screen. "This footage is all about the past. What do you think you found out that makes any difference?"

"You're right about that past footage, Mark. Now look at this." With that, Professor Delta turned off the video player and receiver. He then rolled the table with the apparatus on it to the center of the lab and carefully arranged the equipment. "Now, watch carefully," he said, when everything was in place.

Mark and Flo watched—carefully. Delta seemed to be in his own world—paying no attention to either of them. They looked at each other—confused—until Delta stopped

"This is a sound generator—and this is a what I call a 'sound gun.' The generator produces a specific low frequency sound. A common frequency. One well within the range of human hearing. That sound has always been present—right in front of us. That's probably why no one thought of it before."

Mark grew impatient at what seemed to be evasion. "Okay. But what's the evidence? You haven't shown us anything yet, except some old TV footage that could have come from a science fiction movie. What did you discover?"

"Just watch this." Professor Delta positioned a compass on a small easel, and it showed north—just as it was supposed to do. "This is a standard compass like the ones on most boats and airplanes. Everybody knows how it works. It's very stable and very dependable. Keep your eyes on it." He turned on the generator—which made a soft, low humming sound—picked up the "sound gun" and pointed it at the compass. "Watch."

Mark and Flo looked at the compass. Nothing happened. Then, ever so slowly, the needle began to turn. It moved clockwise for a few moments then counterclockwise. Then it began to pick up speed. Soon it was spinning—fast.

"Look at that," Flo said. "Just like the radio and TV reports from the boats and airplanes. The compass has gone crazy! But are you sure it's because of the sound? Could it be something else in here?"

"Watch the compass," Delta said as he turned off the generator.

The needle stopped spinning and returned to its former north reading.

"Wow!" Mark said, staring at the now-still compass. "That's impressive. But is it enough to explain the whole Bermuda Triangle?"

Flo shook her head. "No, it's not. It's an interesting demonstration of a single event. A good parlor trick! You must have much more than this one demonstration. Don't you, Professor?"

"I knew you would do that, Flo. That's exactly why I need—and want—you here. Be a skeptic. Force me to prove it to you beyond a doubt. Then I'll be able to prove it to the scientific community at large."

"Okay then," Mark said. "Let's see what else you have."

"It better be good—and strong," Flo added. "If you can't prove this beyond a reasonable doubt you could become a laughing stock among your scientific colleagues. And you certainly don't want that to happen."

CHAPTER 8

Professor Delta went to the far side of the lab and invited both of them to join him next to a huge tank of salt water. "See that?" he said when he put in a large block of wood. "The wood is floating—just as it should, and just like a lot of wood around here floats. Just like many of the boats around here that were lost to the Triangle."

"So?" Mark and Flo asked simultaneously.

"So watch."

Delta turned on the generator again, and again there was the soft, low humming sound. He aimed the "gun" at the block of wood. They all stared at it.

At first, nothing. But then the block began to move a bit, like the compass had moved. The block of wood shuddered, then it vibrated, and the water around it began to show small waves.

"What's going on?" Mark asked.

"You'll see. Wait just a moment."

As they watched, the block of wood sank to the bottom of the tank.

Mark blinked. "What happened? What did you do? That block of wood just sank. Wood isn't supposed to do that. Wood floats. But that wood sank."

Delta nodded. "Right. The vibrations came from the sound waves—that specific frequency I told you about. The sound waves caused the molecules in the wood to vibrate. The wood then became water logged—and it simply sank. All kinds of wood respond the same way. I took pieces from a lot of local boats, and they all went down—some quickly and some slowly, but they all sank!

Flo gasped. "No wonder some of those old fishermen didn't know what happened to them."

"Right. One minute they had a solid, water-tight craft—and then, in a moment, it was sinking. Did you notice how the water around the block of wood made little waves?"

Mark nodded. "I saw them. Did you, Flo?"

"Yes."

"Well, in a bigger tank with bigger pieces of wood the water really moves—almost like it's boiling—so fast that it creates a mist."

"A mist?" Mark asked. "That's part of the mystery, too. Many times there was a sudden fog reported just before the problems started. The boats and the planes reported being suddenly surrounded by a fog." He was still staring at the block of wood on the bottom of the talk. "I can't believe it. It seems too simple."

"Often, Mark, the most difficult things are simple once they've been explained. The trick is to know what to look for."

"And to know it when you see it," added Flo.

"Okay, Professor, but there has to be more. I remember reading about bigger boats—ships—steel ships—that were lost. Steel wouldn't get water logged like that block of wood." Mark pointed at the block on the bottom of the tank. "Your sound explanation doesn't seem to fit the big ships that went down. What about them?"

"He's right about the steel ships, Professor," Flo agreed. "What about them?"

"I wondered about that, too, Flo. For a long time I tried the 'gun' on small ships made of metal. Nothing happened. "I thought my theory didn't hold water. Excuse the pun. But then I realized the models I was using didn't have something all the real ships had. Separate plates of steel held together by rivets. So I got a couple of steel plates and had a friend at the boat yard rivet them together. When I got home, I turned the 'gun' on them."

"And…" Flo and Mark asked as one.

"The rivets heated up—got very hot—and they popped right out of the plates."

Mark's eyes widened. "If the rivets on the real ships popped out of the plates, they would all come apart, and—"

"—the ships would take on water fast—and sink," Flo said, finishing the thought.

"Yes, they would take on water, and yes, the ships would sink. That's exactly what I concluded."

Mark wasn't convinced yet. "But what about all the oil on board? Oil doesn't sink. It floats on the surface. It would be visible for a long time."

"You're right about that, Mark. Watch this."

Delta poured a container of oil into the tank of water, and, as expected, it floated on the surface. He aimed the 'sound gun' at the oil slick on the surface of the water and increased the volume on the generator.

Again there was a soft, low hum.

As they looked at the oil they saw it shudder a bit, and then it slowly sank to the bottom.

They all looked at each other.

"Looks like you're right Professor," Mark conceded.

"I agree," Flo added. "The 'gun' makes everything happen that happens in the Triangle."

"What a story this is going to make," Mark stated. "I'd better call the office. We should get a crew here to take pictures and shoot video. I'll—we'll—be famous, and soon. What a scoop!"

"Wait a minute, Mark. The scientific journals get this before the TV news."

"Come on, Professor. This is big stuff. It can't wait for the scientific journals to drag their feet all over it."

Flo shook her head. "He's right, Mark. He should have the chance to tell his colleagues about this before it goes on the tube and all over the Internet. We have to do more data checking to be absolutely certain there is no other explanation. Then all the data should be peer reviewed before it's released."

"Oh. Not you, too, Flo. This is my big chance."

Flo laid her hand on Mark's arm. "But I still have plenty of questions before we can give full support to this finding. It's one thing to aim a 'sound gun' at a piece of wood and make it sink, but where's the 'sound gun' in the ocean? That's where the real Triangle is. It's not in a tub of water in the lab."

"You're right, Flo. Sound waves in water travel just like they do in the air—only much faster. They bounce around when they hit things—rock walls, coral reefs, boulders, all sorts of things down there. And then they change direction. They also respond to temperatures. Did you know that, Flo?"

"I didn't know that. Now? What happens?"

Delta opened a large chart to help with the explanation. "Well, when sound waves hit cold water they go down. And they continue going down until they hit something that makes them bounce up—like the ocean bottom. Or, they might come in contact with warmer water. If the sound waves are strong enough, and the angle is sharp enough, the bounce makes them turn upward toward the surface. If they're really strong, they could even go right into the air!"

Flo blinked, slowly processing these implications. "And if there happens to be a boat—or an airplane—in the path of the sound waves, they'll react just the way these models did in the demonstrations in the tank."

"Right."

Now Mark was caught up. "Yeah, but where does the sound come from? I don't think we'll find any generators or amplifiers, or 'sound guns' down there."

"There are all sorts of sound sources under water—some natural—some manmade. Volcanoes are constantly erupting under water. And many frequencies in those eruptions are the same as those I produced with my 'sound gun.'"

CHAPTER 9

Delta spread the chart on the table and pointed to the section of the ocean near where they were located. "Look at this. The explosives some companies use in underwater excavating could produce these same frequencies, and I suppose they could cause those same effects. Man-mad explosives produce frequencies just like the volcanoes do—the same ones produced by the 'sound gun. Now couple those sound waves with the water wave action and the tides and currents in the ocean, and you could induce the same results we saw here in the lab—but on a much greater scale!"

"How can you be sure about the wave action underwater?" Flo jumped in. "I've never seen anything like this in my area of research, so this is all new to me. That part about temperature bending the sound waves—and the sound bouncing around. Is that theory, or do you have proof?"

"Here, again is an example of looking at something for a long time—and then suddenly seeing it. Look at these pictures." Professor Delta put a tray of slides in his old carousel projector and dimmed the lights to produce a clear, sharp picture.

Like Professor Delta himself, it had been around for a long time and had worked hard through numerous lectures and scientific presentations. Visual technology had advanced dramatically over the years, but again like Delta the standby of the old slide technology still worked—well.

The first slide was an underwater scene, showing what looked like a smooth path in the sand.

"Look at how this 'path' seems to have been swept clean on the ocean floor? Sound waves did that." Delta clicked the remote and another slide appeared on the portable projection screen. "The rounded stones you see here are constantly moving. They are regularly 'bombarded' by sound waves moving through that same course—that same channel—over many years. These findings have been available for a long time, but it's just recently that I saw them as part of the Triangle explanation. These pictures were all taken here in the Caribbean. Not far from where we are right now." He pointed to the map. "Here's where those cleanly swept channels are."

"Then the sound wave movement in the water here is constant."

"No, Flo. Not constant, but consistent—and persistent. It's been going on for a long time."

"So has the Triangle mystery," said Mark.

Prof Delta studied the map. "Right. But now I'm convinced we know what has been causing all those accidents."

Mark couldn't contain himself any longer. "Professor, I'll make a deal with you. You get your findings ready for publication. I'll call the office and tell them we're about ready to release a blockbuster story. I won't give them any details—or even hints—only that it concerns the Bermuda Triangle. That will get them to send a crew, for sure. Everybody likes that science fiction stuff. No offense, Professor. I mean the scientific findings. Your sound wave theory is interesting—but the Triangle is real *news*!"

"He's right, Professor," Flo joined in. "I agree that the journals should have this information—and you should have the reaction and support of the scientific peer community, but Mark's TV coverage will help make this information even more profound and interesting—to everyone not just your colleagues. Besides, we could save lives and property by releasing the information. That'll help boat and plane crews plot courses and avoid the dangerous conditions—and it will protect fishermen with small boats, too."

Without a word, Professor Delta rolled up the map, put it back on the shelf, and walked outside. He sat down on the steps and put his head in his hands. Obviously, he was thinking about what might be the best thing to do. Mark and Flo opened the map and looked carefully at notations on it that defined the underwater channels.

It was almost a half hour before Delta came back into the lab. He had made his decision. "All right, Mark. Call the station."

CHAPTER 10

Mark was on the phone, talking so fast Flo and Delta just looked at each other, shrugged their shoulders, and smiled.

He was like a little boy with a secret and a new toy, and he couldn't wait to tell someone—everyone—about it. He was working hard to give enough information to capture the interest of the person he called but not too much to break his word. He was talking to his editor. "...that's right, The Bermuda Triangle. I can't give you the details on the phone, but I can tell you this. You better get a crew down here ASAP. This is BIG!" There was a long pause while he listened. "If that's the best you can do, three days will work fine—but no longer. The professor needs time to get his notes together anyway. If his findings leak out, we'll lose the best story we've ever had. Every TV and radio station, every newspaper and blog will be all over this story. For now, it's all ours! So let's make the best of it." He paused to listen again. "Good. I'll get everything we'll need for the story— background, bios, charts, maps. I'll set up interviews with boat captains, man-on-the-street stuff. Everything." Silence ensued for a few moments. "Okay. Good. See you then."

He hung up and clapped his hands. "What a story! They're all going crazy trying to figure out what it is."

"Then let's get started," Delta said with the calm demeanor of a scientist. "There's plenty to be done. Flo, will you review all those notes in the file cabinet there in the corner? We have to be sure there's nothing missing in the explanation. I'll organize the photos, the computer print outs, and some of the video I shot. You haven't seen any of that yet, but you should. Mark, listen and start making notes. You'll have a great story to tell, and I know you want to be sure not to miss anything."

During the following two days, each of them concentrated on their individual responsibilities. Delta realized he had more paperwork than he thought, and the piles began to grow.

Flo concentrated on the computer notes, often having to stand up, rub her eyes, and take lots of walks to stay mentally sharp. The sheer volume of data was almost overpowering, but focusing on the scientific details was absolutely necessary.

Mark had set up an "office" workspace in the far corner of the lab, and it quickly filled up with charts, time-lines, pictures, and a host of different-colored sticky-notes.

No question about it—the story and the documentation were all coming together. When the TV station crew arrived the next day, they would be ready for them, and then the action would begin.

All three of them were in the lab late in the afternoon when the phone rang.

Delta answered. "Yes. This is Professor Delta. Yes, he's here. Can I tell him who's calling? Right. Just a moment. Mark, it's for you. Your news director."

Mark took the phone. "Yeah, Frank. What's up? I expected to hear something from the crew this morning. I thought they'd be here by now."

There was a long pause along with a look of disbelief and confusion. "What? What do you mean they aren't coming?" Mark said. "This is the biggest story we've had in years, and you expect me to cover it alone—without a crew?" His expression showed even more confusion and disbelief. "You must be kidding. You can't be serious! You don't even want me to cover it alone? How can you say there's no story? I told you what I saw and what Professor Delta found out. You can't mean it!" He clenched his fist as he listened to what was coming through the phone. "Well, we'll see about that," he said after a brief silence. "Yeah. I'll see you when I get back—with the story."

He hung up, looked at Delta and Flo, and then he fell into a chair. "Can you believe that? He said 'don't cover the story.' He said there is no story. I'm not supposed to write anything. If I didn't know Frank better, I'd think there was some kind of cover up going on here. But that can't be. Can it?"

Flo was almost as surprised as Mark was when she heard the news. She put her hand on his shoulder for a moment. "What are you going to do?" she asked.

"I don't know right now. I need a little time to figure this out. I'm going out for a while."

Delta tried to keep the stiff upper lip. "Okay. We'll keep at it here. See you in a little while."

He and Flo continued reviewing the charts and other documents as Mark walked out the door.

Mark was disappointed, confused, and angry all at the same time. "I don't understand this at all," he said to himself. And then he punched the wall, but it didn't do any good. He didn't have a plan. He just walked, but soon he found himself at the waterfront—right at dockside. An old fisherman was repairing his nets, and Mark watched him for a few minutes. His hands seemed to move all by themselves. Every move was fluid and smooth—just like the water in the harbor.

The old man watched Mark, too. "My name is Juan, mister. Pretty day, yes? You on vacation? Is nice place for vacation. Where you from? You want to go fishing? I take you. What is your name?"

Mark wasn't really listening at first, but the old man seemed nice enough so he shook his head. "No. No. I'm not on vacation—not really. And I don't want to go fishing. Sorry."

Juan continued mending his net, and looked at Mark. "It's up to you. Good boat. Sunny day. Good water—nice and calm. No problems today."

Mark's attention suddenly kicked in. "What do you mean no problems—today? Have you had trouble on these waters?" He was trying to probe without leading Juan in any particular direction. "That looks like a sea worthy boat. What kind of problems could you have here with that?"

Juan stopped working and smiled. "Not with the boat, mister. She's good. But sometimes the water is funny—does crazy things. But today not crazy. Today is okay."

Mark was getting impatient now, "What do you mean crazy? Do you mean there's something strange with the water? Something funny?"

Juan used his sleeve to wipe his forehead. "It sort of jumps around sometimes. Even on a calm day, the water goes crazy all of a sudden. Bumpy. I had a friend once who had a boat—just like this one. He told me one day the water went crazy on him, All of a sudden. And his boat just sank—like that—" He snapped his fingers then shook his head for a moment and continued to talk. "He always took good care of the boat. Just like me. But all of a sudden, it was gone! He was almost gone, too. He got picked up by another boat, though. He's okay, but he doesn't like to fish anymore."

Mark worked hard at remaining calm as he continued to probe for more information. "Does this crazy water happen all over?"

"No. Just in one special place I know of."

"I'm interested in crazy things like that," Mark said trying to remain calm. "Can you take me out to where this stuff happens?"

"No. Sorry, mister. Not enough gas. Can't go."

Mark took money out of his pocket. "I'll buy the gas—and pay for your time, too. Here."

Juan hesitated before taking the money. "Why are you so interested in this water? It is just water. You Americans are the crazy ones. But if you want to go out there. I'll take you. Sure you don't what to go fishing, too?"

"No. No fishing. I just want to look around."

Juan gathered up his nets and put them in a locker. They both got on board. Juan stated the engine, and they eased over to the dockside gas pump. With the tanks full, they headed out toward the open water.

A couple of other fishermen on the dock had been watching and listening as best as they could from a distance. As Juan pulled away, they looked at each other.

"We better make a phone call—now," one of them said. "This might not be so good."

"Yeah," the other one agreed.

The two of them walked to the end of the dock and went into a little bar. One of them went into a phone booth while the other ordered drinks. The one on the phone began to wave his hands around. He was excited about something.

Juan and Mark were now far off shore. The water was calm—hardly any movement at all.

"Well, mister, this is where it happened."

Mark raised his hands to shield his eyes from the bright sun and the reflections from the water. "I can't see anything strange. Everything looks fine."

"That's the way it always looks—until—until the water goes crazy."

Mark kept looking in all directions as Juan steered the boat in a wide circle. Almost two hours had passed "We've been here a long time, Juan. Are you sure this is where it happens?"

"This is the right place. I'm sure."

Mark looked at his watch—then up toward the sun. "It's getting late. We better head back."

"Okay, mister. We go back now."

CHAPTER 11

Mark admired the skill Juan displayed in handling the boat, and he smiled as he remembered a line he had read years earlier in a boating magazine while waiting in a barbershop. The line read, *Never approach a dock faster than you are willing to hit it.* Good advice. Juan had just demonstrated that skill to a tee.

He maneuvered the boat slowly, and, as it touched the dock gently, Mark jumped off on to the dock. He secured the lines as best he could. Even though he wasn't a real sailor, he thought he had done a pretty good job. Juan watched, but said nothing. When he stepped to the dock, he re-tied all the lines. He didn't want to embarrass Mark. After all, he had just been paid well for an easy afternoon on the water. *What a way to make a living*, he thought.

When all was secured, Mark looked at the bar at the end of the dock. "Thanks for the ride. Can I buy you a drink?"

"Yes, you can."

When they got to the bar, they found a small table, and Mark ordered two beers. There was no air conditioning, of course, but the shade was welcome, and the light breeze felt good.

Mark lifted his glass toward Juan. "So that's all there is to it? It just happens? And it happens at that same spot all the time?"

Juan acknowledged the toast and raised his glass in return. "That's all there is to it. It just happens. Thank you for the beer. It tastes very good on such a hot day." When he put down his glass, Juan pointed to another patron. "Ask him. He saw it too. Almost lost his boat." Then he waved to the other man. "Hey, Charlie. C'mon over here."

When Charlie came to the table, Juan stood, shook hands, and began introductions. "Meet my friend, Mister..." He paused. "Funny. I do not know your name, Mister..."

"Mark will be fine. Hello, Charlie."

Mark signaled for another round of beers then looked at Charlie. "Juan tells me you saw some crazy things out there on the water a while ago. We were out there for most of the afternoon but didn't see anything strange today."

Charlie put down his glass. "It's not there all the time. But when it happens, you know it."

"What happened to you? Juan told me you had bad trouble."

"I sure did. Damn near sank my boat—and me. The water just started to bubble. The radio went crazy. Couldn't talk to anyone. Couldn't hear anything but static. Then the compass started to spin like a top. It got real foggy. Couldn't see anything. I didn't know where I was—or what was happening. I thought I was a gonner."

Mark just looked at Charlie in silence until he was ready to talk more.

"Then it stopped. It was all over. Just as fast as it started—it ended. "

"And then what?"

"Then what? I got the hell out of there! That's what. And I haven't gone back there since. Juan is crazy to go out there. So are you. I ain't never going there again. There's plenty of other places to fish. Thanks for the beer."

With that, Charlie got up and left making it clear he didn't want to talk about it anymore.

Mark watched Charlie leave then turned to Juan. "I don't know. This is weird. I want to find out more about this."

Juan pushed back from the table. "It's up to you. I must go now. Thanks for the beers."

CHAPTER 12

Mark took a notebook out of his pocket. He wanted to make a few notes—and capture a few questions and ideas before they disappeared from his head. When the bartender looked his way, Mark signaled that he was ready for another cold beer.

He was still writing when the beer arrived, and, as he lifted the bottle, he saw that a piece of paper was stuck to the bottom. He thought it was just something left from the bar, but he noticed there was writing on it. He was curious, and then surprised, and then angry when he read the message. *This ain't any if your business. Don't try to make it any. For everyone's good, leave it alone—and leave the island—NOW.*

He looked around quickly to see if he could figure

out who had written it. No one was looking his way. There wasn't a clue who sent it.

He took only a fast sip of the beer, put some money on the table, stood up, and left quickly. He had a bad feeling about this whole thing. It wasn't just about crazy water. There was much more going on. He didn't have a clue what it could be, but something was wrong.

As soon as Mark got to Professor Delta's, he raced to the room he was sharing with Flo. She had just finished showering and was drying her hair. "Well, welcome back. It's about time. Where have you been? We were worried about you."

He fixed a drink—a stiff one, this time—for himself and one for Flo. "You won't believe what just happened. I met this old fisherman. He knew about the strange activity on the water. We went out on his boat to where all those things happened. We were out there all afternoon, but nothing happened. Nothing! When we got back to the dock, we went for a drink. After Juan, the old fisherman, left, I ordered another beer and look what was stuck to the bottom of the bottle"

He handed the note to Flo and took another gulp of his drink. Flo read the note and looked at Mark with disbelief and surprise. "I don't believe this. It must be some kind of joke."

"I don't know about that. But I know it isn't a joke. Why would anyone care if I went out trying to find out about those strange events? How would anyone even know what I was looking for? Juan didn't talk to anyone. We were together all the time. This is really spooky!"

The phone rang, and Flow moved quickly to answer it. "Now what?" She lifted the receiver. "Hello. Oh hi. Frank. How are you? Good. Yes. He's right here. Hold on." Bewildered, she handed the phone to Mark. "It's for you. It's Frank."

"Good." Mark took the phone from Flo, and she went into the other room to get dressed. He took another sip before he said anything. "Yeah, Frank. Change your mind? What? When? Why?" After a pause, he continued. "C'mon, Frank. You can't be serious! Look, it's bad enough you don't want me to cover the story—a big story—but now you're telling me to get right back to start working on a stupid BS story? No way! What the hell are you up to? Who told you to pull me off the story—to not even cover the story at all? You covering up something?" He shook his head. "Yeah. That's what I said. Covering up! What's with you? I've never seen you do anything like this in all the years we've worked together." He listened with clenched fists then exploded. "Then that's it. Screw you!"

He slammed down the receiver, took another drink— a much longer one this time—and a deep breath. "That son of a bitch just fired me! There must be something going on down here we're not supposed to know about. Frank isn't like this. Someone's leaning on him."

Flo had come back into the room by now. "Who would do that? And why?"

"Damned if I know. But I'm gonna find out. I want to talk to Professor Delta again."

They left the room and headed for the lab. Both Mark and Flo realized they were looking around—for something—someone. They both had a funny feeling they were being watched, but they saw nothing out of the ordinary. They hurried over to the lab. Professor Delta was at the door.

As soon as they got inside Mark showed Delta the note. "Look what I got. What do you make of this?"

"I'm at a loss. Any clues at all about who wrote it?"

"None. Nothing at all."

Flo sat down on the sofa. "Professor, if we knew more about what's going on we might be able to figure out why someone doesn't want Mark to do this story—or even do any more investigating. Do you remember Joe Farns? I saw a newspaper story about him a couple of weeks ago. He's leading a research project not too far from here. It's for the Oceanographic Institute. He might be able to help us—if we can track him down."

"I can take care of that." Prof. Delta went to the phone, placed a call, and waited. After the few moments it took to make the connection, he began a conversation with someone on the other end of the line "Yes. Joe Farns. Right. A research vessel. Can you help? Good. We'll see you in about twenty minutes. Thanks." He hung up and looked at Mark and Flo. "That was Ken Smith with Ropa Industries here on the island. He says Joe Farns is about a half-hour flight from here. Ken's meeting us at the airstrip with the company helicopter to get us out to the research ship."

They all looked at each other with the same question Delta voiced.

"Why is he doing all of this? He doesn't even know us. It's Joe who owes me a favor. Ken's calling Joe right now to tell him we're on our way. Maybe we'll learn something out there. We better get going. Ken will be waiting for us at the heliport."

They left the house and got into the car. Prof Delta drove to the landing strip because he knew the island and the roads better than Mark or Flo did, and there was no time to waste getting lost somewhere.

CHAPTER 13

As soon as they arrived at the small heliport, Delta parked at the operations building. He, Mark, and Flo got out and ran to the waiting helicopter. They were crouched over and holding on to their hats because the rotor was already turning.

It wouldn't take long to get it off the ground.

Delta introduced everyone all around. They shook hands, and Ken motioned for everyone to get on board. Flo led the way, then Mark, then Delta, and finally Ken who closed the door and signaled to the pilot they were ready after all their seat belts were secured.

The helicopters that took the tourists for sightseeing tours around the island were well insulated and almost noise free inside. It was possible to carry on a conversation with only a little extra effort. This helicopter, however, was for work. No frills. Without headsets and microphones, it was impossible to hear anything over the roar of the powerful engines—both the rotor and the stabilizer.

The rotor speed increased—and so did the noise. The chopper fought gravity for a moment—won—and lifted high and quickly into the air. The pilot turned toward the open ocean and the helicopter took them out over the water.

Right on schedule, Ken pointed out the window. "There is it." And they could see the research vessel off in the distance. "Should be on board in just a few minutes."

The pilot brought the chopper close to the landing platform at the stern of the ship and slowly descended until the landing pontoons made contact with the deck. He cut the power to the engine, and the noise level went down quickly. When the rotor stopped, Ken opened the door. "Here we are. Welcome aboard. Here comes Joe Farns."

Everyone exited the helicopter and headed toward Joe, who was hurrying to greet them. "Glad you made it so fast. I was really surprised when you called, Professor. It's good to see you again. And Flo, Mark, it's been a long time. I can't remember our last visit." A strong gust of wind knocked them off balance for a moment. "Let's go below where we can sit and talk."

Ken shook his head. "I can't stay. But thanks anyway. I have to get back to the island for a meeting later this afternoon. Take care. Good luck. I'll be back for you this evening, but if you need me sooner just give a call."

He returned to the helicopter, waved, and the rotor began to move fast. The helicopter rose, turned, and headed back toward the island.

Joe started walking. "This way."

The office area was small with just enough room for the four of them to sit around a steel table. This was clearly a work area.

When the visitors were seated, Joe went to the head of the table. "Now what can I do for you? You sounded concerned about something interesting. What's going on?"

"You're going to find this hard to believe so let me set the scene," Delta began. "This is about the Bermuda Triangle. We know what causes it." That got Joe's attention. Delta nodded. "Let me start at the beginning."

During the next fifteen minutes, they all contributed to the details of the story, form Delta's experiments to the note Mark received and the fact that he was fired from his job.

Flo finished the recap. "…and that's why we came out here. What do you know about all of this?"

Joe just shrugged his shoulders. "Nothing really. We haven't been working in that area at all. And there certainly hasn't been anything like that out here. Look, we've just about finished our research here. In fact, we should be wrapped up by tomorrow afternoon. Why don't you just stay on board tonight? Tomorrow, we'll head down that way to see what we can find out. We have plenty of clothes and equipment and other gear on board—even SCUBA gear if we need it. Wet suits, dry suits, re-breathers, mixed gas. You name it, and we'll have what you're looking for."

Prof Delta smiled. "Sounds like a good idea—as long as there's room and we're not interfering with your schedule."

"There is—and you're not. Now, let's eat, then I'll show you to your quarters. They're cramped—but they're clean. I'll radio Ken and tell him not to bother coming back this evening."

With that, they all stood up, and Ken directed them to their respective cabins.

CHAPTER 14

It was early morning. The sun reflected fire off the surface. It was going to be a hot day. Everyone was already on deck. The ship was under way in a calm sea with a light breeze coming across the bow. Joe was on the bridge, scanning the surface through a pair of powerful binoculars. He was moving constantly, looking for anything and everything that might be of interest and importance. When searching the ocean surface, the trick was to look for something that shouldn't be there. Today there was nothing out of the ordinary, and that was always good news.

He turned to Mark. "From what you told me, Mark, this is where you were with the fisherman. But I sure don't see anything strange."

Suddenly, about a hundred yards off the port bow,

the water began to shimmer. It was gentle, but something was making the surface move. A circular area about twenty yards in diameter looked like a slowly boiling pot of water. And the pot was now moving toward the bow of the ship.

Joe was still looking through the binoculars. "What the hell is that?"

Now everyone was looking at the "boiling" surface. The water became more agitated as the ship moved closer, the rough surface expanding as the ship closed the distance. The bow was now almost at the outer rim of the disturbance. They all braced, grabbed hold of the railing, and waited for contact.

Something was certainly wrong now! But there was no contact. Then they saw the cause of the disturbance. It wasn't anything like the Bermuda Triangle activity they had expected. It was a school of baitfish swimming close to the surface. They saw a couple of dolphins surfacing and diving again as they caught their breakfast, and the baitfish didn't want to be any part of it.

Everyone breathed a sigh of relief as they passed over the fish and past the dolphins. They laughed, knowing that, although they were ready for action, they were happy not to see any.

Relieved for the time being, they all went below.

As they finished breakfast, Joe offered a plan. "The baitfish were fun, but maybe the best way to get to the bottom of this search is to get to the bottom. We have a submersible on board that can take us down. Let's put it to work. We might be able to get a lead on this from down there." He pointed to the water, then to the submersible. "It's ready to go if you are. It'll be tight quarters, but all four of us will fit."

The responses came from all three of them at once, "You bet." "Great." " Let's get going. I've been waiting for a chance to try out that thing."

They climbed into the submersible and got settled. Joe did a radio check. Satisfied that all was in good shape, a crewman closed and secured the hatch. A crane lifted the vehicle off the cradle, and it was smoothly shifted over the side of the ship. When it was clear, the crane operator slowly lowered the submersible into the water.

The safety divers in SCUBA gear disconnected the securing cables and signaled to Joe. "You're clear. Go on down."

At the controls, Joe gently eased the submersible downward. "Here we go. Keep a sharp eye open."

The underwater visibility was about one hundred feet. Good, but not great for this location this time of year.

Joe steered them in a pattern of ever widening circles, moving out from a fixed point directly under the ship.

Mark was getting annoyed and impatient. He turned

away from the porthole where he had been searching the bottom. "Why are we just going around in circles? We're wasting a lot of time looking at the same things over and over again. Let's move on"

Now Joe was annoyed. "We're not looking at the same things. Each search circle has a greater diameter so we're covering new territory all the time. This is SOP—Standard Operating Procedure—when conducting this kind of search. This way we can be sure we're not missing anything. Be patient, Mark." He checked his watch. "We've been down almost an hour now, but there's nothing out of the ordinary here. It's time to go back up, anyway. Let's move the ship to another location and try again later this afternoon."

"That makes sense. Let's go up," Flo said, taking one more look out of the porthole as Joe navigated the submersible back to the surface.

Since the submersible was pressurized and they were breathing air at surface pressure they didn't need to ascend slowly or worry about calculating decompression time. The Bends wouldn't be a problem for anyone.

The crew raised the vessel out of the water, placed it back on the cradle, and opened the hatch. The four of them got out. Joe reminded then they would dive again after lunch. The crew would take care of changing the location and be ready for the next dive as soon as they were.

A new face appeared. Janie, Joe's senior associate, greeted them and introduced herself. "Not so fast, Joe. We might not be moving after all. Not around here anyway." She handed Joe a piece of paper. "This message came over the radio while you were below."

When he had read it, he balled it up. "Bull!"

He handed the paper to Prof Delta who unwrapped it and read the message aloud. "'From the Deputy Secretary of the Interior, Washington, D.C. You are hereby advised that your presence in these waters is unauthorized. You are to leave the area immediately. The research vessel is ordered to return to your assigned study area. Repeat, you are to leave this area immediately.'"

Their facial expressions spoke volumes for all of them. The message was clear, but they had plenty of questions about it.

"What's this all about? Who sent this? Why?"

"Can they do that? Make us leave?"

Joe had a quick answer for Mark. "Hell no. Washington has no authority over this area—or over this vessel, for that matter. This doesn't make sense."

"The operator said it came directly from the Department of the Interior," Janie said. "It looks official as Hell to me."

Mark was about to explode. "This whole thing doesn't make sense. First I'm told not to cover a story I had already been told to cover—then we're told to get off the island and leave the investigation alone—and now the feds tell us to get out of the area altogether."

Flo just shook her head. "This is too much of a coincidence. Professor, do you have any ideas?"

"I'm afraid not. I'm at a loss. But it looks like we're going to have to move away. Flo, Mark, I'm sorry. I brought you down here for nothing."

Joe wasn't buying any of this. "Like I said. Bull! No one's going to tell me where I can take my vessel—or the submersible either. This is open ocean. Those damn feds might think they can shove us around, but they're dead wrong. There's something strange going on here, and we're going to find out what it is. This is a research vessel, and by God, we're going to do some research!"

Mark raised a fist and bumped Joe's. "Now you're talking. Where do we start?"

"We already started! Let's take another look at these charts and set up a formal research pattern. This is more than just your sound wave theory, Professor—much more, and we're going to find out what the Hell it is."

For the next three days, they continued the search, moving the ship, lowering the submersible, finding nothing but pretty fish and colorful coral.

Inside the sub, on the fourth day, Joe was at the helm and Flo, Mark, and Professor Delta were looking out separate portholes so they wouldn't miss anything. The horizontal visibility was now about 150 feet—good for the search.

Flo was dejected. "I don't know, Joe. This is the fourth day in this area and still nothing. Maybe it was just a coincidence, after all. Maybe we should just give it up and go back home. What do you think, Professor?"

Suddenly there was a loud *Bang*. The sub shook, and water began to spray through some broken seams. Everyone was wet, and the lights began to flicker.

Joe was the first to react. "Trouble. We've got to get up fast. Mark, close off those valves. That should slow down those leaks and keep the water out long enough to get to the surface safely and connect to the hoist. I don't want to lose this sub—or anyone on board either." He picked up the mic and told the on-deck crew, "Get ready. Hook us up fast." Then he turned to those in the sub. "This is gonna be close. Hold your breath. Not really, but keep your fingers crossed"

Fast work by the crew and luck all around resulted in the submersible being safely secured to the cradle, and the four of them climbed out. Flo shook out her hair. "That was close. I like the water, but not that much of it and not that fast."

Janie came over from the submersible, holding something. "Look at this fitting. It's been sawed almost all the way through. That's what gave out and made that 'bang,' and let the water in. This isn't normal wear and tear. This was sabotage. Someone wanted to be sure you didn't find anything—or talk about anything you might find."

Joe examined the valve. "This is no coincidence. Someone cut this deliberately."

"But who would do such a thing?"

"I don't know, Flo. It certainly wasn't someone on this crew. We've all been together for a long time. It must have been done when we were docked yesterday for supplies."

Flo voiced what the others were thinking. "Someone tried to kill us! Why, Joe?"

"That's a good question. And we're gonna get some answers. As soon as we can make repairs, I'm going back down. We're all going!"

CHAPTER 15

All four of them were looking through the portholes again, searching for any clues they could find that would explain the strange events. If they had been tourists on vacation, this would have been an exciting dive for them. Colorful coral and multiple rainbows of tropical fish were everywhere. All peaceful and serene.

But they weren't tourists, and this was no vacation. The sabotaged valve was ample proof of that, but why would anyone do that?

Mark was scanning, trying to take in every part of the scene in front of him. "Maybe we'll get lucky this time. We haven't been in this area before."

Joe was looking out of the porthole on the opposite side of the submersible. "If we don't, we'll move to another location—and another—and another—until we find the cause of the weird events. I don't like the idea of those SOBs trying to kill us. I want to find out who's doing it—and why."

Mark suddenly sat up straight. "What the hell is that?"

They all looked in the direction he indicated. Flow was the first to react. "I don't believe it!"

Joe was still angry. "You better. It's for real. We're going to just hang still here for a while and watch. I want to find out what's going on here."

They were looking at a large structure—a man-made habitat of some kind anchored to the sea floor. There was a strange logo painted on the side. The structure was in a deep depression. With coral stands surrounding it, it was almost completely hidden. If their viewing angle had been different they would have missed it. Divers in strange looking gear were working on something near the bulkhead, and small submersibles were moving throughout the area.

"What do you make of it, Joe?"

"Beats me, Flo. I don't know for sure yet, but I have a few thoughts. Let's get around to the other side for another view."

He eased the submersible into motion, staying close to the bottom to avoid being seen, and kept the sub moving slowly so they wouldn't stir up any sand to give away their location. They kept a close watch on the divers and the other subs. The entire scene was filled with activity.

Suddenly, Joe stopped their forward movement. "I'll be damned! They're digging for something! From old charts I've seen of this area, they must be looking for wrecks. There have been a lot of them over the years—centuries, but salvage diving is never attempted here—for anything or by anybody"

Mark was still peering out of the porthole. "But why here? And why that underwater factory?"

"Because, like I said, no one has rights to dig here. No one! If there were a salvage site here with the usual surface vessels, everyone would be able to see it—and stop it—or interfere with it. To 'invade the site.' But this way, no one knows what's going on down here. Every pirate and scavenger in the Caribbean would be here, taking whatever they could get their hooks on. It's amazing how quickly word gets out when there's a possibility of a treasure find. It's impossible to hide a ship here, but a ship can't be seen if it's on the bottom."

Professor Delta turned to Joe. "But working under these clandestine conditions, there could easily be an accident that could wipe out all the people working down here."

"Right, Professor." Joe started moving the sub again—still very slowly. "Let's see what we can find out. If they do all the work here—cutting, polishing, setting gems, and distributing gold and silver—they could make a fortune. There would be no way to trace the source or the owners. For all intent and purposes, this place doesn't exist. No one knows anything about it. Except the ones responsible for the structure, the ones working on it—and us now!"

They stayed at a distance but brought out binoculars to get a better look.

Mark got out his video camera to record as much as possible. "No one is going to believe this. And if we're being chased away by someone, we better have some documentation to support what we see. With the feds involved, we could be in big trouble, and we better have plenty to show and talk about."

What they saw surprised them. Large equipment was being moved to locations marked by small flashing light beacons. The divers were guiding the equipment and positioning probes of some sort into the sea bottom and the surrounding coral. A large warning sign on the side of the largest piece of equipment warned "Explosives."

The divers anchored the movable piece of equipment over the probes that had been set. Then they positioned large deflectors called "mailboxes" over the "explosives" unit. Such deflectors were often used to direct the path of a blast caused by an explosive detonation. Without a mailbox, the blast wave from an explosion would travel outward in all directions from the blast location. With the mailbox, the blast wave could be contained and aimed in one direction.

Mailboxes were often used by salvage crews, even on the surface. The large units were tubes, shaped at a right angle. On the surface, the top portion was attached to the stern of a ship, and the thrust of the props was directed into the top of the tube. A ship was anchored in place and the props started and run at high speed—sometimes at maximum speed to produce maximum thrust. That thrust could be aimed in any direction by moving the tube. The resulting thrust could move sand, rocks, coral, and fish—anything in its path.

When everything was in place at the salvage site, the divers moved into the habitat, and all the submersibles left the area. The mailbox deflectors had been placed to direct the blast wave safely away from the habitat/work area. In this situation, on the bottom, the engine props weren't being used to create thrust. The crew was using explosives

Everything grew still. Something was going to happen—soon.

Professor Delta turned from the porthole. "That's it!"

"What's it?"

"A blast—and those deflectors. That's what caused the action on the surface. That's your Bermuda Triangle!"

"Hold on Professor. You're not making sense," said Mark.

"Yes, I am. Now it all makes sense. The sound

waves in the explosives contain the same low frequencies I showed you all in the lab. The water concentrated the sounds, and those deflectors directed them."

Mark wasn't convinced. "But we're pretty deep. That explosive charge couldn't get to anything on the surface."

The sand had been moved by the sound waves, making a path like you could see on a snowy street after a snowplow had gone through.

Flow had been listening, but suddenly she bolted upright in her chair. "Wait, Mark. I think I see what's happening." Then she turned to Professor Delta. "Those sound waves went along the bottom because of the deflectors, and they stayed there until they hit something— like a coral wall—and they bounced up toward the surface. If you look carefully at the bottom there, you can see the paths the sound waves have made on the sandy bottom. Just a casual look wouldn't detect them, but once you see them, you can't miss them."

Delta nodded. "Right. Just like a beam of light bouncing off a mirror."

"And they were focused and concentrated enough to get to the surface and cause all that strange activity."

"Right again, Flo. And if there happened to be something in the area—a boat or a plane—those strange things happened to it—Bermuda Triangle things!"

"And if nothing was there, no one would know anything about the explosions, Mark chimed in. "It would just have happened, and ended." That's why someone wants us out of here," he said, after a long thoughtful pause. "We saw their secret."

"And that's why we have to get out of this sub and back on board. We're sitting ducks down here. We'll stay deep until we get far away from here. No sense taking a chance on letting anyone see us now." Joe checked the compass heading and set a course that would take them back to the ship "We'll stay close to the bottom until we get to the ship then surface on the far side—just in case someone might happen to be looking this way. When we get back on board, we have a lot of things to figure out, and, from the looks of all the activity here, we might not have much time before the secret gets out."

It didn't take long to get back to the ship. It just seemed long because they all were eager to get to work on figuring out what to do.

The ascent was smooth. When all the cables were attached and secure, the sub was lifted gently out of the water. Fortunately, the sea was still calm so the retrieval was uneventful. Rough seas made for uncomfortable retrievals.

With the sub secured, Joe opened the hatch and made a quick safety check. Everything looked good so, one by one, they squeezed out of the tight opening and jumped down to the deck.

"I'll finish shutting down the sub while you all start changing clothes," Joe said. "I'll get cleaned up and change. Let's plan to meet in the dining area in a half hour. Will that work for everyone?"

They all agreed and headed off to their cabins

A little after the half hour had passed, they were all together.

"I just called a friend in DC," Mark said. "He's going to find out who's been doing the digging around here. I told him about the logo, too, and he thinks he can trace it down quickly through a friend at the trademark office. He'll get back to me as soon as he can."

Professor Delta had been in deep thought while Mark was talking. "You know. I could swear I've seen that logo some place before—but damned if I can remember where."

"Well, Professor," Flo said, concern evident in her voice. "Let's hope we find out soon. I have a bad feeling about this whole thing. Now, let's recap what happened today and figure out what questions we have to find answers for."

CHAPTER 16

Later in the evening, a couple of hours after dinner, they were in the lounge—each one in thought, trying to sort out what had happened—working to separate fact from fiction. There was something strange about the situation, and they were all struggling with the same questions.

"Why the underwater explosions?"

"Who is responsible?"

"What are they looking for?"

Janie had joined the group, and she was the one who jumped when the radiophone rang. "This is Research One. Go ahead, please." As she listened, she began to frown and looked toward Mark. "Okay I'll put him on." She handed Mark the handset. "It's for you. It's your friend in Washington."

As Mark reached for the handset, Joe intercepted it. "Put it on the speaker so we can all hear this."

Janie set the switch and nodded to Mark.

"I'm here," he said. "Go ahead."

Everyone listened intently to the voice coming from the radiophone. "Mark, you really got on to something—or into it. I'm not sure. That logo you told me about is registered to a conglomerate called Ropa Associates. They have offices all over the world—including Bimini!"

Delta jumped to his feet. "That's where I saw it."

"And now for the BIG news," the voice on the radio continued. "One of the associates—one of the managing partners is Duane Donner."

Mark was now on his feet, too. "Who the Hell is that?"

"None other than the deputy secretary of the Interior. That's who. The guy who wanted all of you out of the area."

"And he probably got to my boss at the station," Mark shouted.

"Probably. That guy has plenty of clout. He's a bad ass—and I hear he's on his way down there right now." After a brief pause, he continued. "I think you're in for a visit soon, pal, and I'd be careful if I were you. You guys know a hell of a lot—and he could have a lot to lose. He might be desperate, and who knows what he's capable of doing? I'll let you know if I find anything else. Good luck. Out."

Mark shook his head in disbelief. "Thanks. Out."

Janie took the handset from Mark and switched off the radio speaker and the main power. They were all quiet—trying to figure out what to do next. Because of their varied experiences, they were all coming at the situation from different perspectives—Mark as a reporter looking for the truth in a story, Joe as a researcher and a sailor, Flo as a biologist, and Delta as a scholar. None of them had ever had any experience with crimes of any sort. No one had any idea of where to go or what to do next. They were all thinking out loud.

"Damn," Mark said.

Joe nodded. "You said it."

"Now what?" Flo asked.

"I have no idea." Delta cocked his head. "What's that?

A low "thumping" sound could be heard. It continued to get louder and grew as the moments passed.

Joe looked out the porthole. "This might be your answer now."

Everyone headed for the open deck and saw a helicopter heading their way. It was low and moving fast. It flew around the ship to get the best wind, and everyone on the deck could see the corporate logo. Ropa Associates was coming for a visit.

The helicopter hovered above the landing pad on the rear deck for a moment and then gently touched down.

The engine was turned off, and, as the rotors slowed down, the door opened. Ken and three other men jumped down to the deck.

The newcomers joined the others on deck.

"When I left I said 'Take care,'" Ken said. "You didn't. You got into something you should have left alone—left to the fish and the superstitious fishermen all around here. You got in way over your head and opened up something that should have been left alone before anyone got hurt."

Joe couldn't believe what he was hearing from his old friend. "Ken, we've known each other for years. What are you doing? How could you get involved in this sort of thing? Illegal salvage?"

Ken ignored the question but pointed to one of the other men who had been on the helicopter. "This is Duane Donner. I think you probably know who he is by now."

Donner looked at the group long and hard. Clearly he wasn't ready for a friendly conversation. "You were told to leave the area. You were warned. Now you know too much. We have too much invested—and too much at stake—to just let you go."

Mark stepped forward and got in Donner's face. "What do you mean? Are you threatening us? This is international waters. You can't force us to leave. You can't be serious about all of this."

Donner returned Mark's stare. "Oh but we are serious—dead serious. You simply can't leave now."

Joe was reaching his breaking point. "And just how do you plan to keep us here? A lot of people know exactly where we re. They'll be looking for us—and they'll find us. They have plenty of equipment for that. And they'll find you, too."

Donner just smiled and nodded his head. He looked like he was having a good time, even as he was threatening all of them. He didn't seem to be bothered a bit. "You're right. A lot of people do know exactly where you are—right in the middle of the Bermuda Triangle! We don't have to worry about keeping you here or anywhere else. You see, you'll just disappear—exactly like a lot of other people and ships have disappeared over many, many years. That's what happens in the Bermuda Triangle. Things—and people disappear. You'll all just become another set of statistics added to the mystery. In a way, you'll all become a part of history. I bet you never expected that to happen, did you? Professor Delta, especially, will probably receive a number of pages in the history books that will be written. He was the academic researcher who became a victim of the very mystery he was studding. Rather dramatic, don't you think?"

"So, you see? You'll have to stay here now," Ken added, pointing down to the water. "Right there."

Mark was back in Donner's face again. "Just how do

you expect to get away with it?"

Ken once again jumped up and did the talking. "Very simple." He pointed to the man sitting in the helicopter. "Amos over there is going to pilot this vessel out into deeper water. We have a powerful version of a sound gun on board—you're very familiar with that aren't, you Professor? But yours is a toy compared to this one! When we get to the designated spot, we'll direct the sound signal at this vessel, and, in no time, you and the ship will just sink. No trace at all. Just another victim of the Bermuda Triangle! Nothing and no one will ever be found."

Ken began to bark orders. He seemed nervous and anxious—as if he wanted to get this over with and move out of the area before anyone saw the ship. "Now let's get started. Bert. Tie them up. Amos, take the wheel and get this vessel to the point I marked on the chart. We'll follow in the chopper—and pick you up when you get to the location."

Bert tied them up—just as he was told to do. Mark put up a bit of a struggle, but a sharp punch to the side of his face stopped that quickly. When all of them were safely secured, Bert climbed onto the chopper along with Ken and Donner. The chopper lifted off the deck, banked to the left, and headed farther out to sea—to the position Ken had selected.

On board the ship, Mark shook off the punch and began to work on freeing himself. He remained out of sight from Amos who was at the helm guiding the vessel to the designated location. He had no idea what Mark was do-ing.

About twenty minutes had passed. Amos again checked the chart and throttled back on the engines. The ship would move slowly, but it wouldn't get very far. To any rescue effort—if there ever was one—it would look as if something bad had happened to the engine. Then he disconnected the ignition switch. They were right at the designated location.

The chopper was just above them, and Amos signaled to be picked up. When it touched down on the deck, Amos climbed on board. He buckled in, and the chopper lifted off again, leaving the ship moving very slowly—almost adrift. If the ship was ever found they didn't want an anchor overboard. The ship had to look as if it were under way when an "accident" happened.

Mark was finally free and quickly began to untie Flo. Together they untied the others.

Flo rubbed her wrists. "Okay. So now we're untied. What do we do? Amos made sure we can't stop the engines. We're adrift."

From up above, Ken's voice crashed on to them from the speaker on the hovering helicopter. "I really hate to do this. But you had plenty of time to get out of this area when we told you to leave. You gave us no choice but to sink the ship. Unfortunately, you'll have to go down with it."

The chopper was swinging back and forth above the ship, and a low humming sound came from the speaker. It was the sound gun.

Ken's voice overtook the humming of the sound gun. "You might already hear the sound gun warming up. It will take a few minutes to get it to full power. Then it will all be over quickly. You probably won't feel much for very long and then—it's over! I'm sorry it has to end this way, but you gave us no choice."

He stopped talking, and the humming of the sound gun grew louder.

Back on the deck of the ship, Joe opened a storage locker. "We have one chance. If it works. Janie, get that signal mortar there and set it up on the deck. Mark, get me that trolling cable from that locker in the storage area below deck."

They had no idea what he was planning, but they moved quickly doing what he told them. When the mortar and the cable were positioned on the deck, Joe attached the cable flare to the mortar. He aimed the mortar straight up.

The chopper continued to swing back and forth above the ship. The sound continued to get louder.

Everyone watched Joe.

"That mortar isn't going to knock down that helicopter," Flo said. "Even if you're lucky enough to hit it. You're wasting your time. We have to get off this ship and move away, or we won't have a chance of surviving that sound gun when it reaches full power."

The sound continued to get louder.

Joe continued to adjust the mortar and the cable. "You're right, Flo. The mortar won't—but the cable might—if we're lucky. Anyway, we get just one try."

Ken's voice now boomed from the helicopter. "The gun's almost ready, so you better say your prayers. This won't take long."

Joe's eyes focused on the helicopter. He adjusted the motor trajectory and shouted over the rotor noise. "No. You get ready."

With that, he fired the motor. The round jumped into the air, pulling the cable. The mortar shell passed the helicopter, and everyone on board the ship groaned in disappointment. Everyone, except Joe. He knew his plan was working. The mortar round passed the rotor blades, but the cable got caught. The helicopter began to gyrate out of control as the tightening cable slowed the engine.

The pilot couldn't keep it steady. It slowly turned up on its side and lost altitude. The rotors hit the water. A blade broke off and hit the fuel tank. A powerful explosion rocked the ship. It stayed afloat, but the helicopter hit the water hard and sank quickly. There was no sign of any survivors. Between the explosion and hitting the water hard, all on board were lost.

On the ship, everyone had turned away from the explosion, but now they turned back to see what had happened. Only the tip of one of the rotor blades was visible. Everything else was already underwater—sinking quickly.

Joe was already reconnecting the ignition switch. "Janie, let's get this ship moving and get back to port. Call the authorities, and tell them want happened. Tell them to meet us at the dock. Be sure to get a solid fix on our location here, so we can direct them to the exact spot. They might be able to find something. The water is deep here, but rescue divers might get lucky."

CHAPTER 17

The entire group was assembled in a well-appointed office. Safe, sound, and clean, they had completely recovered from the ordeal and narrow escape a month earlier.

A man named Spencer joined them "I've been authorized by the secretary," he said, in a deep professional voice, "to, first of all, thank you for the job you did uncovering that illegal—and dangerous—salvage operation. It has been stopped. We are now fully aware that your activity started with a scientific inquiry. Professor Delta, your work with sound waves; Flo, your work in the area of bio-physics; and, Joe, your contribution as a marine investigator made this activity possible. It is the decision of the department that the habitat which was built for commercial purposes should be turned over to you for scientific research. The underwater station should be of value to your investigations and research."

Everyone was stunned for a moment, and then the silence was broken by loud cheers.

"Ropa Associates, of course, has agreed to this," Spencer continued. "And the habitat is now under the direction of the Baltimore Aquarium. Professor Delta, it is our hope that you will serve as director, and that you, Flo will agree to be the principal researcher and liaison between the habitat and the aquarium. Mark, sorry, but we really don't have a specific assignment suited to your talents."

"Don't worry about me," Mark said with a big grin on his face. "This story about the solving the mystery of the Bermuda Triangle will be in all the news, and I'll be telling it. Just you watch. But it won't include details of the salvage operation or downing the helicopter. Even for a news person like me, some things should not be revealed—ever."

Spencer gathered up his papers and stood up. "That concludes our business then. Again Thank you to all of you for what you've done. And Good Luck."

After they all shook hands, Spencer left, and the others sat back down silently thinking about what they had gone through and what was ahead for all of them.

CHAPTER 18

Professor Delta, Flo, Mark, and Joe were back on board the ship, and Delta was working to get details firmed up in his mind. "With the habitat and all the equipment down there, we'll be able to continue the research on the Triangle effects from sound waves. Hopefully, we'll be able to chart the sound channels and try to control—or prevent—any more 'Bermuda Triangle' disasters."

"We can't keep people out of the area completely," Flo offered. "But we can develop early warning devices that'll help. And we might also be able to do some underwater excavation to direct the sound to areas where it will do little harm."

"You two have a lot to do, and I'll be around on the

ship when you need a helping hand or a ride in the submersible," Joe added.

"After all this, what I need is a vacation," Mark chimed in with a bit of his usual humor.

"That's what got us into this in the first place," Flo added. "Where would you like to go?"

"Well, we got as far as 'C' for Caribbean when the phone rang. Let's see, 'D.' How about Death Valley?" A long pause. Flo just looked at him, and Mark sighed. "Naa. I guess not. How about 'E'?"

"Just keep looking, Mark. Just keep looking."

About the Author

J. Robert Parkinson has served as a communications consultant and coach for numerous Fortune 500 companies working successfully at all levels of corporate, government, and academic institutions from CEO's to new hires.

In addition, he has taught more than 1750 communication related programs for clients in the U.S. and internationally and consulted and conducted research in South America, Africa, and Australia. He earned a PhD degree from Syracuse University. His other degrees are: MA in Management and Supervision, and BA in English and Biology from Montclair State University (NJ).

Writing extensively for publication, he has had nine books published in the US. One of his books, *How To Get People To Do Things Your Way*, has been translated into eight languages. His most recent books, *Becoming a Successful Manager, Executive Briefings & Presentations*, and How to Get Others To Do What You Want Them To Do, are available on Amazon.com and in major book stores.

For two years he wrote a weekly newspaper column, "Business Speak" for the Milwaukee Journal Sentinel in Milwaukee, WI, and for the past five years he has been writing a similar column titled, "Show and Tell" for the Sarasota [FL] Herald-Tribune.

He served as host of For Your Consideration, an award-winning weekly radio program in Chicago. He hosted a similar television series, The Learning Curve, and co-anchored North Shore TV News. In addition, he has written, produced, and hosted television programs for CBS, NBC, and in dependent productions. After serving on active duty in the U.S. Army, Parkinson began his professional career as a high school English teacher. Later he was appointed to positions as a principal and in central office administration.

Professional positions include: Faculty and Director of School of Speech Intern Program, Northwestern University; Director of Research, Governor's Office, Springfield, IL; Director of Research, Bell& Howell Co., Chicago, IL; Director of Research, Supermarket Institute, Chicago, IL (now Food Marketing Institute, Washington, D.C.); Associate Dean/Teacher Education, National Louis University, Evanston, IL; Dean, Center for Research, National Louis University, Evanston, IL.

Parkinson lives with his wife, Eileen, in Sarasota, Florida.